Betty Bib's
FAIRY
FIELD GUIDE

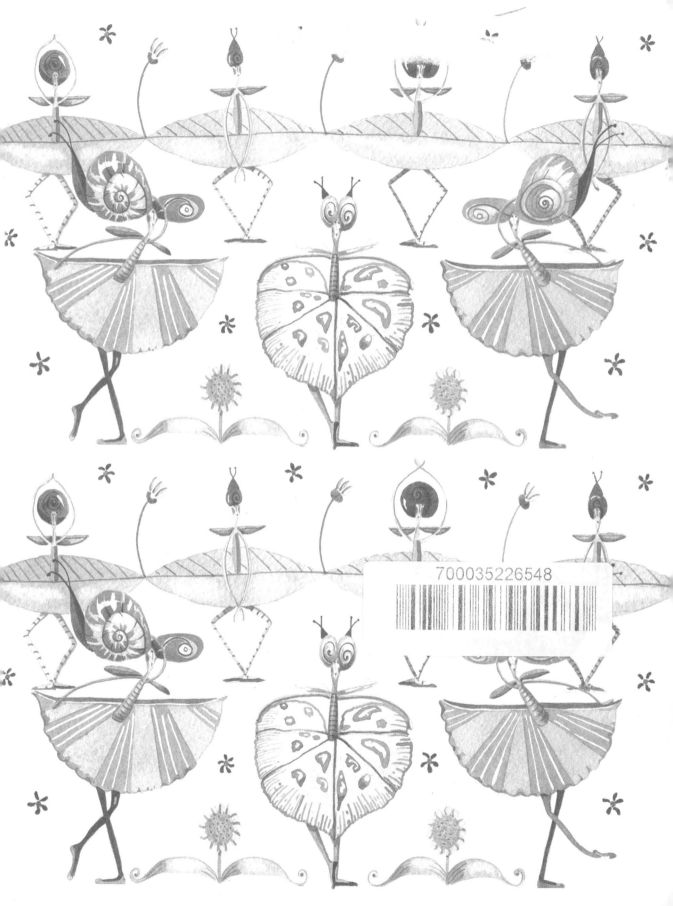

Betty Bib's
FAIRY
FIELD GUIDE

The Illustrated Handbook of Fairies and their Habitats

dbp

DUNCAN BAIRD PUBLISHERS

LONDON

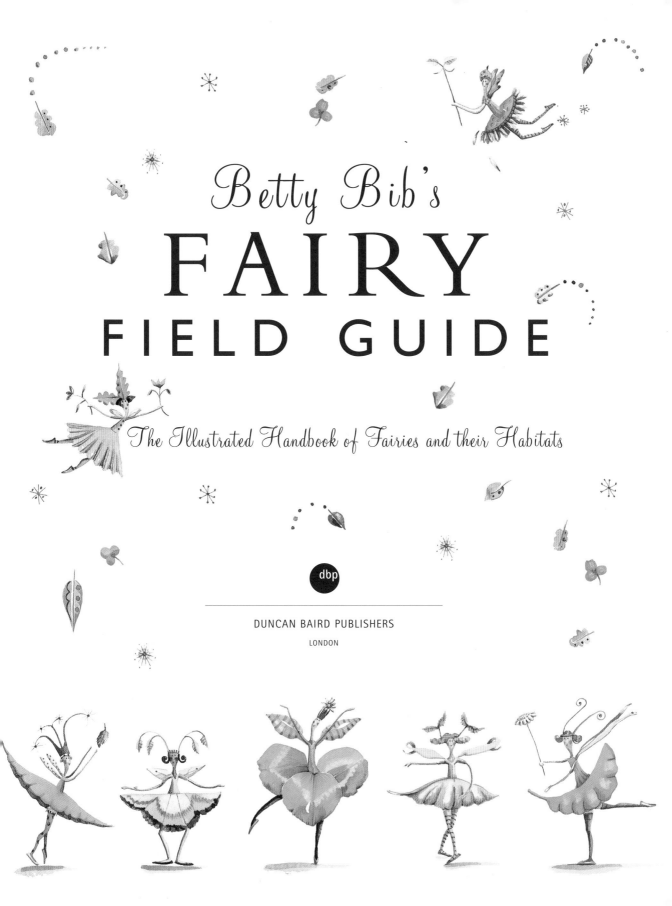

Betty Bib's
FAIRY
FIELD GUIDE™

To Betty and Dennis – a rare breed of parent

First published in the United Kingdom and Ireland in 2005 by
Duncan Baird Publishers Ltd
Sixth Floor
Castle House
75–76 Wells Street
London W1T 3QH

Managing Editor: Kirsten Chapman
Editor: Ingrid Court-Jones
Managing Designer: Manisha Patel
Designer: Rachel Cross

British Library Cataloguing-in-Publication Data:
A CIP record for this book is available from the British Library

ISBN-10: 1-84483-150-7   ISBN-13: 9-781844-831500

3 5 7 9 10 8 6 4

Typeset in Perpetua and Monterey
Colour reproduction by Colourscan, Singapore
Printed in China by Imago

Betty Bib ™

CONTENTS

P. U. F. F.

Dear Reader,

It has come to my attention that very few people in these modern times have ever seen a **fairy**! Nor it seems have they collected a broken wing or fallen wand — I find this quite **extraordinary**. And so, as a celebrated collector of all things fairy and as an expert in the field, I have written this book to educate you all in fairy ways and so increase your chances of spotting some of these **magical creatures**.

Fairy numbers are, sadly, in decline. And this is largely a result of our **carelessness**. For example, nature fairies have been seriously affected by pollution and pesticides. But they are not the only threatened species. There are many other kinds of fairy sharing in our everyday lives who suffer because of the ignorance of the **general public**. It is my hope that with a little **education**, you may be able to help in small ways to produce a healthier environment for fairies and so increase their numbers.

Of course, some **foolish people** say that there are no such things as fairies. Well, I say **pooh** to them, for in the following pages you will see **real fairies** posing alongside my own watercolour sketches of fairies that I have observed.

I hope I am not **blowing my own trumpet** if I say that I am one of the **few people** whom fairies trust to be involved in the great cause known as P.U.F.F., which, of course, stands for Promoting the Understanding of Fairy Folk. Indeed, it has become my **vocation** to share my knowledge of these little people from **the Other Realm**, so that in these fast-paced, technological times we can pause to honour their **quirks** and **customs**, thereby increasing the **magic** in our lives.

Yours most cordially,

Betty Bib

Common Fairy Queries

On my travels around the country lecturing on behalf of P.U.F.F., I have encountered a good deal of curiosity about fairy folk – such as what they look like, where they come from and their different types. This chapter shows you how to use this book and gives you my answers to the most commonly asked questions about fairies.

I once saw a dozen Fun Fairies dancing on the back of my dachshund Dorking — and what's more, he didn't seem to mind very much!

HOW DO I SPOT A FAIRY?

Because fairies move very quickly and they are clever at disguising themselves, it isn't easy to spot them. But if you take the trouble to learn about fairy ways, practise sitting very still and allow yourself to feel the fairy magic, you may attract some of these enchanting little visitors. To help you to gauge how easy it will be to see various fairies, I have devised some symbols which will appear throughout this book – see the Key to Symbols below.

ARE SOME FAIRIES RARER THAN OTHERS?

Many fairies, such as the General Domestics, are surprisingly common, but some are rare or even endangered. In my experience the "Thank-you" Letter Fairy is in sad decline, but perhaps the rarest of all in these throwaway times is the Handkerchief Fairy. (I always check old handbags in the faint hope of finding a trapped and forgotten Handkerchief Fairy.)

WHAT ARE FAIRIES LIKE?

Like people, fairies have different temperaments. Many, such as the Sock Fairy, are full of mischief and enjoy playing tricks. Others, for example the Garden Fairy, are very shy by nature. And still others, such as the Make-up Fairy, love adventure.

HOW BIG IS A FAIRY?

This, of course, depends on the type of fairy. For example, a Thimble Fairy is far smaller than a Candle Fairy; a Seed Fairy can be as tiny as a pin, whereas any royal fairy can be quite large, with the Fairy Queen reaching a height of 9in/230mm.

KEY TO SYMBOLS

STATUS			CHARACTERISTIC			WINGSPAN

| Common | Rare/ endangered | Royal | Mischievous | Shy | Adventurous | inches / millimetres |

WHAT DO FAIRIES LOOK LIKE?

Fairies dress to blend in with the environment. So it is that you will find Sweetie Fairies dressed as bonbons and General Domestic Fairies who look like maids. One of the most attractive fairies is the Fun Fairy, whose job it is to create merriment and mirth. She looks rather like a circus performer and can be identified by her sparkly tights.

FUN FAIRY

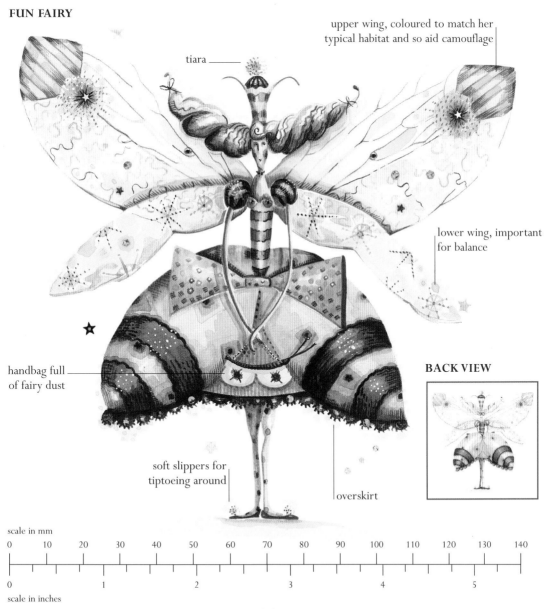

tiara

upper wing, coloured to match her typical habitat and so aid camouflage

lower wing, important for balance

handbag full of fairy dust

BACK VIEW

soft slippers for tiptoeing around

overskirt

scale in mm

0 10 20 30 40 50 60 70 80 90 100 110 120 130 140

0 1 2 3 4 5

scale in inches

Beach Fairies sunbathing in a sardine tin (July, early morning).

WHERE DO FAIRIES SLEEP?

Fairies need very little sleep – only about one hour a day, which they take in the form of frequent, short naps. Ideal sleeping places include: flower-pots (keep them clean to encourage a fairy visitor); shoe boxes (use shoetrees if possible, as fairies like sleeping under them); and biscuit tins (clean out the crumbs as they get caught in fairy hair). Of course, it is at night, while we are sleeping, that fairies are at their busiest.

a matchbox ...

a nutshell ...

a ring box ...

a seashell ...

Fairies can fit into very small places. They might hide or take a nap in ...

... or a little tin.

MAKES DELICIOUS BEEF GRAVY IMPROVES ALL FOR DISHES

OXO BRAND CUBE

a small box ...

1 3

Love Baby

Strawberry Baby

Chubby Baby

Shy Baby

Cry Baby

Bow Baby

Star Baby

Lace Baby

Button Baby

WHERE DO FAIRIES COME FROM?

A baby fairy begins life as a speck of fairy dust that floats down to Earth on a sunbeam and then embeds itself inside the head of a golden dandelion. Her first wand is a dandelion seed. The only exception is a royal fairy baby who descends into a rosebud and has a golden stamen as her first wand.

Baby fairies come in all shapes, sizes and colours, as you can see from my "collection" opposite.

When the flower matures into the seedhead, the baby fairy can be seen at its centre.

HOW DOES A FAIRY GROW?

A baby fairy grows quickly, gaining weight from sipping dandelion milk, which is very rich in nutrients. After about seven days, she is ready to float away into the wide world, clutching tightly to a dandelion seedhead.

She is born with the innate ability to find other fairies and she very quickly makes friends. She weans herself on pollen porridge and dried lavender husks. When she weighs about as much as an acorn, she takes her first cup of honeydew which gives her the strength to grow a fine pair of silky, gossamer wings.

HOW DOES A FAIRY LEARN TO FLY?

The next important stage in a fairy's life is when she learns to fly.
This she does on the backs of butterflies, dragonflies and, in the colder months,
migrating birds. Although to the casual observer this may look like fun, it is also
a vital phase for a fledgling fairy – flying through clouds, skimming water,
looping-the-loop, and negotiating crevices and keyholes at speed
require patience and pluck.

Baby fairies caught on film playing with the stars (November, cold night, full moon).

WHAT DO FAIRIES NEED TO KNOW?

A fairy loves to look her best at all times, and so as she grows she learns all about health, hygiene and general grooming. Of course, she also has a more formal education which takes place among the buttercups and daisies. This includes studying serious subjects, such as the names of plants and the languages of insects, as well as how to predict the weather from the shape of the clouds and the whispering of the grass. However, the most important task in a fairy's life is to spread fun and magic around her.

Fairies learn this from the simple act of playing, and you can often observe young fairies linking arms to make daisy chains, or trampolining on cobwebs or rolling about in thistledown.

When a fairy discovers the magic in the sound of a seashell, in the patterns of snowflakes and the fragrance of flowers, she knows that it is time to receive her magic wand and become a fully-fledged fairy.

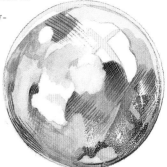

Fairies grow up to be vain creatures. They develop the trait as babies through admiring their own reflections in bubbles and water.

Any handy vessel, such as a clean bird bath or a leaf filled with rainwater, will make a suitable bathtub for baby fairies.

Fairy Directory

To become a fully-functioning, grown-up fairy, a novice must first attend the Great Wand Ceremony in the Other Realm, which is presided over by the Fairy Queen herself. During the ceremony the novice is granted her one and only wish – to choose what type of fairy she would like to be. Along with her fairy vocation, she receives her tiara, her gown and her wand of stardust. Then, adorned in her new finery, she flies back to Earth to carry out her duties as a fully-fledged fairy.

In the following pages of this Fairy Directory, I shall tell you about a variety of fairies that you are likely to see if you pay more attention to the little things in life.

It is a moving moment indeed when Audrey the barn owl and I watch the novice fairies fly off beyond the moon to the Other Realm to receive their "grown-up" wands from the Fairy Queen.

Collection 3
Domestic Fairies

General Domestic Fairy

Dust Fairy

Normal Peg (for scale)

Clock Fairy

Bathroom Fairy

Fairy Peg

Tea-time Fairy

Use beeswax polish in your home to attract domestic fairies.

DOMESTIC FAIRIES

No home is too humble for the domestic fairy. Whether it's an apartment, a chalet, a bungalow or an igloo, the domestic fairy adapts to any altitude or temperature. Fairies love to share in our everyday lives. Many, such as General Domestics, lend a helping hand; but others, such as Dust Fairies, can be rather a hindrance – in their enthusiasm, they often scatter more dust than they clean up (but then fairy dust does sparkle so beautifully in sunlight). And Clock Fairies, who are meant to ensure that clocks keep good time, often can't resist swinging on the hands, making them fast or slow or stopping them altogether.

 ### FORAGING FAIRIES
(Scoffa omnia)

Foraging Fairies are very useful to have around. It's their job to sweep up forgotten crumbs, which are just the right size for a fairy snack and make a good base for a fairy trifle. So don't worry if you drop a few morsels here and there, because you're actually helping to keep up fairy numbers.

 ### BATHROOM FAIRIES
(Hygenica triumphalis)

In my travels as an ambassador for P.U.F.F., I have discovered that 95 per cent of males believe in at least one fairy: the Bathroom Fairy – an industrious little creature who restores order in our smallest room on a regular basis. Strangely, however, it seems that far fewer females believe as fervently in this fairy.

SOCK FAIRIES

(Hosiera pungentia)

Sock Fairies are common creatures, and if you are the puzzled owner of some odd socks, then you can be sure that you have been visited by a few.

Of course they mean very well, but, being rather disorganized fairies with short attention spans, they soon slip from sorting into cavorting. Before very long they can be found playing "hide and snip", a game that involves burrowing down a sock and snipping their way out of the other end – heel or toe, they don't seem to mind which.

NEEDLEWORK FAIRIES

(Pinnit etstitchita)

Recognizable by the bows in their hair, Needlework Fairies are sadly endangered; at one time they were found in every home, but they are now sorely depleted in numbers because of the modern trend of throwing away garments rather than mending them.

These fairies are also suffering as a result of the disappearance of their sewing-basket habitat. Please help to avert this grave situation before they go the way of the dodo, and do, do keep a supply of hooks and eyes, press-studs and pins, and needles and thread. Best of all, take good care of Granny's button tin, which is a favourite haunt of this species.

Needlework Fairies have a habit of collecting leftover thread to make into fairy cloth.

CAKE FAIRIES
(Spongea delecta)

It is a fact, not universally known, that the aroma of a home-baked cake will attract a whole flock of fairies, and even the shop-bought variety will interest the odd straggler passing by. (Fondant fancies, Victoria sponge and, of course, fairy cakes are their favourites.) Fairies will often risk discovery for the ruby gleam of a glacé cherry, the rainbow colours of sugar strands and the twinkle of icing that seems to beckon them to skate over it.

I am told by my Cake Fairy friends that they sorely miss the old-fashioned yet informative practice of labelling plate contents with little handwritten flags such as "cherry Genoa" or "Battenberg" – somehow it gave the occasion an air of importance and festivity. I think if you ever felt moved to revive this fashion you would undoubtedly bring a touch of enchantment and possibly some surprise guests to your tea-table.

Jam and cream are fairies' favourite cake fillings.

FAIRY CAKE RECIPE

4oz (115g) butter or
  margarine
4oz (115g) sugar
2 eggs, beaten
½ tsp vanilla essence
4oz (115g) self-raising flour
2 tbsp milk

for the icing:
4oz (115g) icing
  (confectioners') sugar
juice of 1 lemon

Preheat oven to 200°C/400°F/gas mark 6. In a large bowl, cream the butter or margarine with the sugar until light as a fairy. Gradually beat in the egg and the vanilla essence. Then fold in the flour and stir in the milk. Spoon the mixture into paper cases placed on a baking tray and bake for 15–20 minutes until the cakes are golden brown and firm to the touch. Cool on a wire rack. To make the icing, put the icing sugar in a bowl and add the lemon juice. Beat together until the icing is thick enough to coat the back of a spoon and semi-opaque like a fairy's wings. Spread it over the top of each cake and decorate with one of the suggestions opposite. *Makes 18 small cakes.*

Crystallized rose petals
for a fragrant crunch

Finely chopped lavender
(English or French)

FAIRY CAKE
DECORATIONS

A freshly-picked primrose from
the garden or woodland

A single sugared almond or
a pounded green pistachio

TEA-TIME FAIRIES
(Infusa civilis)

Fairies simply can't resist the magical ritual of a real afternoon-tea: the ruffle of doilies on best china; sugar cubes and silver tongs; a pat of golden butter; and the fragrant steam of a pot of Lapsang-Souchong or, even better, Rose Pouchong — their favourite blend. Please, do not — I beg of you — abandon the use of real-leaf tea. For it is only by its continued enjoyment that Tea-time Fairies will flourish.

There is no finer habitat for a fairy than a satin-lined tea-cosy, although cotton and wool will be tolerated.

TEABAG FAIRIES
(*Infusa vulgaris*)

Of course, as is the way in nature, fairies must adapt or perish. And so, in keeping with our times, a new type of fairy, the Teabag Fairy, has evolved and become much more prevalent than the Tea-time Fairy. (Some might consider her attractive, but personally I find her garb most dull and her manners sadly lacking.)

Oriental Poppy Fairy

Collection 6
Nature Fairies

Leaf Fairy

Pansy Fairy

Water Fairy

NATURE FAIRIES

The fairies of field and forest find life in our world quite difficult, as they fight valiantly for survival in the face of all the pollution and other damage we are doing to our planet. However, there is much that you, the general public, can do to help them.

Do not be put off by the apparent enormity of the task. Remember the fairy motto, "Because the little things matter … " In small ways you can clean up your environment and make our world a better place for fairies. (For example, if you resolve never to drop chewing gum again you will be taking a step toward safeguarding the species – the sight of gossamer wings trapped in this sticky substance is a sorry sight indeed.)

Garden Fairies wear long cotton frocks to protect themselves from stings and thorns.

GARDEN FAIRIES
(Horticultura cultivata)

To a fairy, the smallest patch of soil, from a herbaceous border to a window box, constitutes a garden. As a result, there are a lot of very keen Garden Fairies.

In their behaviour, there are some who like to scatter and sow, and others who prefer to tend and hoe, but all of them are recognizable by their green fingers (which is where the phrase originates). Everything they tend, from a tiny clump of violets to a huge golden sunflower, grows big and strong under their nurturing touch.

Fortunately for us, Garden Fairies also help to deter slugs and snails from nibbling away at our plants, as the fairy dust that they scatter is a natural irritant to these pests' soft underbellies. If you go out at night to pick slugs and snails off your plants, you'll also increase your chances of spotting your resident fairies who prefer generally to toil by twilight.

Look in the corners of greenhouses and cold frames — fairies like a warm spot in which to take a herbal tea-break.

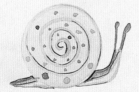

To avoid discovery, a Seed Fairy folds her wings and curls up into a ball.

 ½–3in 12–75mm **SEED FAIRIES**
(Pippa nurtura)

If you manage to see any of these elusive fairies, you'll note the dullness of their outfits. But their plain appearance conceals fairies who are bursting with life. In early spring it's their job to wake up all the trees, shrubs and plants in their vicinity and remind them that it's time to grow. Throughout the following months, these helpful creatures flit from buds to flowers to fruits, checking the progress of their charges, until their seeds are ready to fall. Autumn is their busiest time of year, as these energetic fairies have the responsibility of ensuring that seeds are scattered as widely as possible – a job that can lead to heated squabbles with birds and squirrels. By winter, Seed Fairies are fit to drop and look for a warm patch of earth or a forgotten seed packet in which to hibernate.

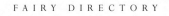

ROYAL GARDEN FAIRIES
(Horticultura regala)

A queen among nature fairies, the Royal Garden Fairy is easily
identified by her extravagant dress, which changes according to
the season. In the picture opposite, she is in her summer display;
in winter, she wears a more sombre moleskin gown and thistledown muff.
Her main duty is to oversee the common Garden Fairies as they attend to
their menial tasks, but she is not above watering the flowers now and then.

Despite the impressive dress and wingspan, the Royal Garden Fairy can
fold herself easily into gutters, cracks in walls and the spaces beneath
flowerpots. I have also observed this fairy sleeping in an abandoned bird's
nest, in a pair of gardening gloves and inside the folds of a faded garden
umbrella. (It had pink and green stripes with canary-yellow fringing
– a Royal Garden Fairy won't settle just anywhere, you understand!)

The Royal Garden Fairy often
has an entourage of insects in attendance.
Look closely at the red and black spots of the
ladybirds — these denote how many years they have
been in royal service.

Fairies have been among us for a very long time, as this Roman fountain testifies.

  ## FADED-FLOWER FAIRIES
(Flora potpourria)

These fairies are tidy creatures who hate to see things go to waste. They work hardest at the
end of summer when they collect fallen petals and leaves, and dried seedheads, which they
gather up into fragrant piles. (As suggested by their Latin name, they were the originators of
pot pourri.) These fairies carry the lingering scent of summer in their petticoats and remind
us that there is beauty even in a fading bloom.

WILDFLOWER FAIRIES
(Flora nopickamea)

Who among you knows that the juice of the Great Celandine (*Chelidonium majus* L) is an effective cure for warts, or that Holly (*Ilex aquifolium* L) is traditionally planted next to houses to protect them from lightning? The Wildflower Fairies are the wise keepers of this dying knowledge. Although, thankfully, they are still quite common, their habitat is under constant threat. To help to keep up their numbers, the only thing you need to do is take the time to identify and appreciate the wild flowers growing around you, and allow them to flourish in their natural habitat.

Of course, spotting a Wildflower Fairy is quite another matter – as they are mistresses of camouflage, these timid creatures can be very difficult to see. As with the other fairy species, there are general Wildflower Fairies and also fairies specific to each plant and flower, such as the Poppy Fairy (left) and the Cornflower Fairy (right).

Many wild flowers open and close their petals at set times of the day. Likewise, a Wildflower Fairy will always be able to tell you the correct time.

ROYAL CLOVER FAIRIES
(Trifolia regala)

Above we see a portrait of a Royal Clover Fairy. She has royal status because the clover plant is vital to the production of the rich honey that sustains fairies in the wild. (And did you know that four-leaf clovers only grow where a Royal Clover Fairy has visited?)

MUSHROOM FAIRIES
(Fungia ballerina)

While out walking Dorking early one morning, I spotted these dainty fairies dancing in the dew. As their Latin name suggests, Mushroom Fairies are graceful creatures. And like mushrooms themselves, they bring light to dark places, appearing fleetingly, and as if by magic. They traditionally sit in circles to whisper their secrets – a habit that gave the name to the Fairy Rings they leave behind them. Fairies also store magic dust in some types of mushrooms, such as Puffballs. Prod one and you'll see!

PRIMULA FAIRIES
(Flora primula)

Primula Fairies are very adventurous creatures – I once saw one sitting on a flower-pot blatantly sipping thistledown tea in full view of a group of humans attending a garden party. Dextrous and bright (both in appearance and character), they are gregarious and sophisticated. (Be careful not to confuse them with their wild, paler cousins, the Primrose Fairies, who are less extrovert but lovely in their simplicity.)

All fairies love to dance, but none more exuberantly than the Primula Fairy, who performs between March and September.

SEASONAL FAIRIES

 ### ROYAL SPRING FAIRY
(Blossomia regala)

You will need to get up early to catch this member of the fairy aristocracy, as she appears at sunrise. She heralds the return of bud and blossom, prepares the earth to absorb the sun's rays and promises the return of longer, lighter days. (Seen only on the Vernal Equinox.)

ROYAL AUTUMN FAIRY
(Harvestia regala)

You can sense the presence of this fairy because she will make you shiver on a warm day. In her wake the leaves begin to crisp and curl as she grants them permission to prepare for their colourful autumnal display. (Seen only on the Autumnal Equinox.)

ROYAL SUMMER FAIRY
(Solara regala)

You should have more chance of seeing this fairy than the other seasonal fairies, as she appears on the longest day of the year. However, she is not particularly easy to spot because she hides under shady leaves to shield her delicate skin from the sun. (Seen only on the Summer Solstice.)

 ROYAL WINTER FAIRY
(Chillitosa regala)

A relative of the Snow Queen, this fairy visits on the shortest day of the year. Her message is one of light, as light must surely follow the darkest hour. Snowdrops appearing in January and February do so only where her fairy dust has fallen. (Seen only on the Winter Solstice.)

Collection 10
Special Occasion Fairies

Valentine Fairy

Christening Fairy

Birthday Fairy

Christmas Fairy

Easter Fairy

SPECIAL OCCASION FAIRIES

In some ways, special occasions were made for fairies, as they combine two of their favourite pastimes: dressing up in all their finery and feasting on rich food. The selection of nibbles, the woosh of a party popper and the sparkle of champagne go straight to a fairy's head. Indeed, I would say that fairies can get quite giddy just on the atmosphere of a good party.

There is a fairy to suit every special occasion, for they love nothing better than to bring their magic to festivals and traditional gatherings. The smallest event that is organized with care and attention will generate a great deal of fairy activity, irrespective of how much money is spent on it.

The same applies to presents. For example, fairies generally advise that giving a small posy of flowers that you know the recipient loves will create more magic than giving them a larger bouquet that you've bought in a hurry from, say, a supermarket (as seems to be a current trend).

Look carefully among discarded gift wrapping and tissue paper — eternally inquisitive fairies like to slip inside parcels, while excitable ones enjoy swinging from gift tags.

These Birthday Fairies' skirts are made of the paper cases in which cakes are baked.

 BIRTHDAY FAIRIES
(Natalicia felicitata)

Birthday Fairies are the busiest of all fairies as, of course, they never have a day off! Perhaps it is because of this that they seek to remind us that a belated birthday wish or card will not have the magic of one that arrives on the actual day.

 CHRISTMAS-TREE FAIRIES
(Arbora Xmas)

A Christmas tree never fails to deliver magic. This is because each one has its own personal fairy who also watches over every aspect of the festivities – Christmastide offers a great opportunity for fairy watching (if you can find the time).

FAIRY-LIGHT FAIRIES
(Illuminata twinkla)

Christmastide is one of the busiest times of the year for Fairy-light Fairies. It is during the shortest and darkest days of the year that we most need these magical fairies to comfort and inspire us. They love the scent of real Christmas trees, and although at one time they were rather picky about nestling in artificial foliage, they have come to accept that some humans find falling pine needles too much of a nuisance. They will now twinkle merrily in any fir or spruce, plastic or otherwise.

Fairies of Asian origin have a long-standing association with lanterns and fireworks and are often to be found at celebrations.

But Christmas isn't the only festival to attract Fairy-light Fairies. The flickering oil lamps of Diwali, the great Hindu Festival of Lights, exert a strong pull on these playful creatures. But they do have to take care not to fly too close to the flames, or they run the risk of a singed wing or two.

In China there are even more illuminated delights on offer: paper lanterns, fire crackers and fireworks send Fairy-light Fairies into a frenzy. The more excited these fairies become, the brighter they glow, until their display rivals anything that humans can produce.

If you are a single and you sleep with a piece of wedding cake under your pillow …

  BRIDAL FAIRIES
(Nuptuala enchanta)

In days gone by fairies had a reputation for making mischief at weddings, so people went to great lengths to avoid attracting them. Traditionally, brides never wore green – the fairy colour – in case they made the fairies jealous. Thankfully, fairies today have much better manners and bring a touch of enchantment to the festivities.

Dressed as little brides, bridesmaids or flowers, fairies mingle most unobtrusively at the reception – sipping neglected champagne and feasting on wedding cake crumbs (although generally they favour softer icing).

When people see a bride in her gown, they often remark "She looks like a fairy bride", little realizing that they are experiencing the aura of magic which fairies give to all women on their wedding day.

.... a fairy will whisper the name of your future husband in your ear.

Bridegrooms are well-advised to leave the ring box ajar on the eve of the wedding, because if a fairy sleeps next to the wedding rings, a long and happy marriage is assured.

And brides should choose their wedding flowers with care, as blooms have hidden powers. From a fairy point of view, an ideal bouquet would include roses for happiness in love, ferns for sincerity, corn for riches, and ivy for friendship and fidelity. And as every fairy knows, carrying a sprig of orange blossom is a symbol of fertility, for orange trees bear plentiful fruit.

Flowers are also usually worn by wedding guests, as "button-holes" on their lapels. Blooms particularly fitting for this purpose include butterfly orchids (for gaiety) and daffodils (for regard).

Collection 12
Stationery Fairies

If you are inclined to hoard your paperwork,
you are likely to attract Stationery Fairies who
like everything orderly — unfortunately, they often lose
vital items in their impatience to tidy.

"THANK-YOU" LETTER FAIRIES
(Gratia multa)

After a special occasion it is most important to send a "thank-you" letter. Sadly, as this nicety seems to be dying out, the "Thank-you" Letter Fairy is in decline. I therefore implore you to take up your pens and finest writing paper and bring back the "thank-you" letter to help to revive the fortunes of the "Thank-you" Letter Fairy. (I'm afraid that an email just won't do as it is highly unlikely to be kept and treasured.)

STATIONERY FAIRIES
(Pencillia etmiscillania)

Another fairy who is becoming endangered is the Stationery Fairy. This is largely because of the disappearance of writing desks – her finest habitat. The smell of ink, the secret drawers, the comfort of a blotter – oh, how these are missed. Stationery Fairies are now migrating in large numbers to offices, which are a far less romantic environment, but nonetheless serviceable, as there is much to interest the discerning fairy in a good supply of paper clips, staples, labels, stamps and other tiny temptations.

This Japanese Airmail Fairy has origami-folded wings — some have wings made from rice paper.

AIRMAIL FAIRIES
(Envelopia wingata)

Fairies will travel any distance over land and sea to safeguard airmail letters sent with love and to keep magic alive between friends or far-flung family.

One of the treasures of my collection is a fairy stamp — seen here greatly enlarged
(the original is the size of a sugar grain).

This is my cat Pastry, who attracts fairies on a daily basis, just by being quiet and content.

How to Attract Fairies

To bring fairies into your life, it pays to study their essential characteristics. At the core of their being is a love of beauty, which is probably why fairies are mostly depicted within the natural world. This is a good place to watch out for them but you must stay very still and "lose yourself".

Having said this I must confess that fairies are also most partial to glitz and glamour – it matters not whether you wear diamonds or paste, a fairy will swoon over all things sparkly. Add to this ribbons and bows, tassels and trinkets, feathers and fripperies and you will have a veritable fairy paradise.

Fairy traps – a cruel invention indeed – were traditionally set with food as an enticement. Although you will never set a trap yourself, I'm sure, it is still worth studying a fairy's diet – for apart from when she sleeps, mealtimes may be the only time when she stays still long enough to be observed.

… WITH SWEET AND TASTY THINGS

Fairies have a delicate digestive system and must be careful of what they consume. Strictly vegetarian, they will eat all manner of crumbs both sweet and savoury – but it has to be said that they favour the former. This may be because they require high-energy fuel – their wings, much like hummingbirds', have a rapid rate of movement.

The appearance of the food is very important to fairies, which probably explains why they are attracted to sweetmeats. Various species of fairies have even evolved from this predilection, for example the Chocolate Box Fairies (who just can't resist installing themselves in the spaces left where chocolates have been eaten), the Confectionery Fairies (who really love the rustle of chocolate wrappers) and the Turkish Delight Fairies (look for their footsteps in the icing sugar), as well as the more health-conscious Fruit Fairies.

This doesn't mean that savoury fairies don't exist – we wouldn't want to omit the Spice Fairies (keep fresh spices in attractive jars to promote these) or the Cheese Fairies (buy hand-made cheese and find them among the folds in the wrapping).

Of course there are many more types of food fairies, but this must suffice for now as an introduction to attracting them into your pantries.

... WITH PRETTY THINGS

Sometimes I am asked why I see no male fairies. Perhaps
it is because they belong to the realms of elves and pixies,
whereas fairies essentially embody the feminine principle.
Some, such as nature fairies, are nurturing and almost
motherly; others, such as domestic fairies, love to restore order
where there is chaos, and cleanliness where there is dirt. But
one basic characteristic common to all fairies is that they have
a distinctly frivolous side, which is aptly demonstrated in
their love of all pretty things.

It is hardly surprising then, that one
of their worst vices is vanity, and

Fairies' hair ranges from fine and neat to wiry and wayward.

few fairies can fly past a dressing table
well-stocked with shiny pots and potions.
For the domestic fairy (as opposed to the
nature fairy) the ultimate environment
in which to linger would be a boudoir.
Unfortunately, few of us can stretch to
our own private haven for primping
and preening, but you can try evoking
a boudoir atmosphere in your bedroom
— and then wait for curious little visitors
to appear. Essential "props" to set the scene
might include powder puffs, pom-poms and
tassels, perfumes, lotions and cologne, combs, clips, pins, and nicely packaged
make-up (if you must buy bumper bargain sizes, do decant the contents into
pretty little bottles).

Please keep the lids on all your powders and blushers
— I once saw a fairy covered in apple-blossom pink
from wing-tip to toe, after she had fallen into an open pot
of shimmery rouge.

Fairies love to hide in the folds of a fan. These have dressed up for
the occasion. They are sad that there are far fewer functions these days
to which they can wear their long satin gloves.

… WITH THE LITTLE THINGS IN LIFE

Fairies are great believers in living in the present, but they still like to honour the past and occasionally succumb to bouts of nostalgia. This means that an amusing way to lure fairies into your life is to maintain a keep-sake box. This might be a faded chocolate box that retains a hint of the cocoa-bean, an ornamental tin or (particularly effective) a box of cedar or any other receptacle that enjoys a certain aroma; and in it you might keep beribboned love letters, a lock of hair, a first shoe or your grandmother's glove – all prime artefacts that fairies love to pore over and peer into.

Another container that exudes a magical aura because of the memories it evokes is the box or tin that holds your family's special-occasion cake decorations. I personally keep a tin with Dorking and Pastry's birthday candles in (as well as a selection of Easter chicks, a plaster snowman, a china Father Christmas and a frosty fir tree, all wrapped up in a cake ruff.) Fairies love all such objects because they thrive on the memories of past parties and festivities.

Any boxes, tins and containers that have nostalgic qualities will attract fairies, so be sure to check them regularly and add new treasures occasionally to maximize your chances of finding little visitors.

Keeping your treasured greetings cards tied in a pretty ribbon (rather than an elastic band) will ensure fairy safety at all times (Valentine's Day, morning).

… WHICH THEY TAKE TO THE FAIRY QUEEN

And if you have ever wondered what happens to all the mementoes that you have lost along life's path, or what became of the trinkets and trivia that made a certain day significant, or if you have ever mourned the breaking of a favourite piece of china, then, take heart. Most probably a fairy has scooped up that doomed brooch with a weak clasp, or that sugar-cube wrapper from the café in Paris or the plastic mermaid from a shared cocktail; and all these prizes have been taken to the Fairy Queen who will treasure them for ever more. Alas, sadly, there is no hope of reclaiming your lost objects, as they are sewn into her ceremonial gowns that are worn only for state occasions on the other side of the moon, in quite another realm.

FAIRY QUEEN
(Regina magicalia)

Her Majesty owns gowns of every hue so that when she visits us she can easily blend into any background. Being much larger than her subjects (9in/230mm) she has to be particularly careful not to be detected. However, her visits are rare as she prefers to send her sisters the May Queen, the Snow Queen and Queen Bee on her behalf. I am therefore extremely honoured to pass on the following message from her Majesty to you, dear reader:

> *"It is with keen anticipation that we hope to see man and fairy come closer together in the giving and receiving of magic and mirth. Our dearest wish is that this little book will serve to Promote Understanding of Fairy Folk (P.U.F.F.) among humankind and, in return, we pledge to Pour Our Love Into Sceptical Hearts (P.O.L.I.S.H.)."*

INDEX

Acknowledgments
I would like to thank Bertie for his
generous support; the creative team at
Duncan Baird Publishers; and Her
Majesty the Fairy Queen for giving
her royal stamp of approval
to this book.